Dear Parent:
Your child's love of reading starts here!

Every child learns to read in a different way and at his or her own speed. Some go back and forth between reading levels and read favorite books again and again. Others read through each level in order. You can help your young reader improve and become more confident by encouraging his or her own interests and abilities. From books your child reads with you to the first books he or she reads alone, there are I Can Read Books for every stage of reading:

SHARED READING
Basic language, word repetition, and whimsical illustrations, ideal for sharing with your emergent reader

BEGINNING READING
Short sentences, familiar words, and simple concepts for children eager to read on their own

READING WITH HELP
Engaging stories, longer sentences, and language play for developing readers

READING ALONE
Complex plots, challenging vocabulary, and high-interest topics for the independent reader

ADVANCED READING
Short paragraphs, chapters, and exciting themes for the perfect bridge to chapter books

I Can Read Books have introduced children to the joy of reading since 1957. Featuring award-winning authors and illustrators and a fabulous cast of beloved characters, I Can Read Books set the standard for beginning readers.

A lifetime of discovery begins with the magical words **"I Can Read!"**

Visit www.icanread.com for information
on enriching your child's reading experience.

JUST SAVING
MY MONEY

BY MERCER MAYER

HARPER
An Imprint of HarperCollinsPublishers

To Sandra and Ronnie Cipolla

I Can Read Book® is a trademark of HarperCollins Publishers.

Little Critter: Just Saving My Money
Copyright © 2010 Mercer Mayer. All rights reserved. LITTLE CRITTER, MERCER MAYER'S LITTLE CRITTER and MERCER
MAYER'S LITTLE CRITTER and logo are registered trademarks of Orchard House Licensing Company. All rights reserved.
Manufactured in the United States of America. No part of this book may be used or reproduced in any manner whatsoever without writ-
ten permission except in the case of brief quotations embodied in critical articles and reviews. For information address HarperCollins
Children's Books, a division of HarperCollins Publishers, 195 Broadway, New York, NY 10007.
www.icanread.com

Library of Congress catalog card number: 2009941830
ISBN 978-0-06-083558-3 (trade bdg.) — ISBN 978-0-06-083557-6 (pbk.)

Typography by Diane Dubreuil
16 17 18   PC/WOR   10 9 8 7 6 5 4
❖
First Edition

A Big Tuna Trading Company, LLC/J. R. Sansevere Book
www.littlecritter.com

My skateboard is old.

It is broken.

I need a new one.

I tell my dad.

Dad says, "You need money.
Do you have any?"

I get my money jar.
"How about this?" I ask.

"You need to save more money
for a skateboard," Dad says.

I say, "I will do chores and earn lots of money."

I make a list of chores
that will make me money.

First, I feed the dog,
but the bag is too big.

I empty the dishwasher,
but the dishes are too heavy.

I clean my room.

Mom pays me some money.

I sell lemonade.

I get more money.

I save lots of money
in my money jar.

Dad says, "You need
a savings account."

Dad takes me to the bank.

We see the manager.

Dad writes on some
bank papers.
I write my name.

They take my money jar.

I am upset.

Dad says, "Don't worry."

They pour my money
into a machine.
It counts my money.

I get a book.
It tells me how much
money I have.

"Hey, Dad," I ask.

"Can I get a skateboard yet?"

Dad says, "Not yet.
You must save more money."

Every day I do chores
to earn more money.

Finally, I save enough money
for a new skateboard.

But I don't want that anymore.
Now I want a Robot Dinosaur.

I say, "Dad, I am so glad
I saved my money!"